STERLING CHILDREN'S BOOKS
New York

An Imprint of Sterling Publishing
387 Park Avenue South
New York, NY 10016

STERLING CHILDREN'S BOOKS and the distinctive Sterling Children's Books
logo are trademarks of Sterling Publishing Co., Inc.

© 2014 by Sterling Publishing Co., Inc.
Design by Jennifer Browning

ISBN 978-1-4027-8349-4

Distributed in Canada by Sterling Publishing
c/o Canadian Manda Group, 165 Dufferin Street
Toronto, Ontario, Canada M6K 3H6
Distributed in the United Kingdom by GMC Distribution Services
Castle Place, 166 High Street, Lewes, East Sussex, England BN7 1XU
Distributed in Australia by Capricorn Link (Australia) Pty. Ltd.
P.O. Box 704, Windsor, NSW 2756, Australia

For information about custom editions, special sales, and premium and corporate
purchases, please contact Sterling Special Sales at 800-805-5489
or specialsales@sterlingpublishing.com.

Printed in China

Lot #:
2 4 6 8 10 9 7 5 3 1
01/14

www.sterlingpublishing.com/kids

SILVER PENNY STORIES

The Pied Piper of Hamelin

Told by Kathleen Olmstead
Illustrated by Sarah S. Brannen

A very long time ago, there was a town named Hamelin. One day, a stranger arrived in town.

The man wore a jacket with bright red stripes and a hat with a feather in it. He also carried a tin pipe. The people called him the Pied Piper.

"I am a rat catcher," he told the townspeople. "For a fee, I will rid your town of all the rats."

The people of Hamelin were excited by this news.

"We would be grateful," the mayor said. "We will pay any fee you ask."

The Pied Piper nodded. He took out his tin pipe and went to work.

The Pied Piper walked through the streets of Hamelin. He played a song on his tin pipe. No one recognized the song. They all watched with great interest.

Rats started to follow him. At first there were only a few rats. After a street or two, there were a few dozen. They all followed the Pied Piper.

By the time the Pied Piper reached the edge of town there were thousands of rats behind him.

The Pied Piper walked into the forest. The rats followed him. Soon, the rats were so deep in the woods they could never find their way back to town again.

The people of Hamelin were very happy. Their town was free of rats! But when the Pied Piper asked to be paid, the mayor refused.

"Why should we pay you?" the mayor asked. "We have no rats. Our problem is already solved."

The Pied Piper was very angry.

"You will not get away with this," the Pied Piper said. "You will be sorry that you cheated me."

The Pied Piper left town but promised to come back soon.

Several months passed. One day, while all the adults were working, the Pied Piper returned. He found the children of Hamelin playing in the streets.

He pulled out his tin pipe and began to play. It was a new song. The children had never heard it before. They followed the Pied Piper out of town.

He did not lead them to the forest. The Pied Piper walked into the hills. All the children of Hamelin followed him.

One little boy walked with a cane and could not keep up. So, he returned to town. He told all the adults what had happened.

"Why did we not pay him?" the adults wailed. "How will we save our children?"

The mayor sent people to search the hills, but they found no one.

Several days passed. The adults were very sad. They had lost all hope they would see their children again. Then, the Pied Piper appeared.

"I will give you one more chance," the Pied Piper said. "If you pay me what you owe me, I will return your children."

"Yes," the mayor said quickly. "We will give you whatever you want."

After he was paid, the Pied Piper took out his tin pipe. He started to play.

The children walked back into town.

Their parents hugged them tightly.

Everyone was very happy once again.

No one noticed as the Pied Piper

quietly left Hamelin.